The
Year
My Mother
Was Bald

The
Year
My Mother
Was Bald

by Ann Speltz
illustrated by Kate Sternberg

MAGINATION PRESS • WASHINGTON, DC

Published by
MAGINATION PRESS
An Educational Publishing Foundation Book
American Psychological Association
750 First Street, NE
Washington, DC 20002

For more information about our books, including a complete catalog, please write to us,
call 1-800-374-2721, or visit our website at www.maginationpress.com.

Editor: Darcie Conner Johnston
Art Director: Susan K. White
The text type is Kidprint
Printed by Phoenix Color, Rockaway, New Jersey

Library of Congress Cataloging-in-Publication Data

Speltz, Ann.
The year my mother was bald / by Ann Speltz ; illustrated by Kate Sternberg.
p.   cm.
Summary: Clare keeps a journal that describes the medical treatments her
mother undergoes for breast cancer, her family's experiences, and her
own feelings and concerns. Includes a list of resources.
ISBN 1-55798-837-4 hc : alk. paper — ISBN 1-55798-888-9 sc : alk. paper
[1. Cancer—Fiction. 2. Diseases—Fiction. 3. Diaries—Fiction.]
I. Sternberg, Kate, 1954- ill. II. Title.
PZ7.S7473 Ye 2002
[Fic]—dc21   2002013964

Manufactured in the United States of America
10 9 8 7 6 5 4 3 2 1

2 8 6 0 4 1 9

A NOTE TO THE READER

This story is based on the experiences of my own family during the year that I was treated for cancer. My daughter Amelia and I hope that this book will take away much of the mystery and fear surrounding cancer and its treatment. We also hope that it will give you an opportunity to express your own feelings and questions about cancer. Do you know someone being treated for cancer? If you do, we urge you to read this book with a parent, or with some other trusted adult. When reading *The Year My Mother Was Bald,* please remember that the feelings expressed in this book are the feelings of one particular child. There are no right or wrong feelings; being able to say what YOU are feeling is what is most important—and most helpful.

Scientists keep making new discoveries about cancer. As a result, the medical community is testing new methods of fighting cancer that could change the way different cancers are treated. When you have questions or need more information, you can call the Cancer Information Service, a free public service of the National Cancer Institute that answers cancer-related questions in English and Spanish. The toll-free number for the Cancer Information Service is 1-800-4-CANCER (1-800-422-6237). The American Cancer Society also has a toll-free hotline at 1-800-227-2345, and its phones are staffed 24 hours a day, seven days a week, by trained cancer information specialists.

Perhaps you've been wondering whether cancer is contagious, or what a tumor is, or why people going through chemotherapy often lose their hair. You will find the answers to these and many other questions about cancer in this book. Maybe you're also feeling confused, worried, angry, or sad. When a parent has cancer, children usually experience many different emotions, like the child in this book. Facts and feelings—we hope our story helps you with both.

–Ann Speltz

*To my daughter Amelia, who so generously allowed me
to draw upon her experience in creating the character of Clare,
and to all the healers—family, friends, and health
professionals—who helped to make me better.* —AS

*To my mom, Toddy Soble Sklarsky, who taught me courage
and the power of love during the year when she was bald.
And to Ann and Amelia, for giving me the words, to Darcie
and Sue, for giving me the chance, and to my family,
for understanding why.* —KS

This is the story of the year my mother was bald, and it begins in June. My mom and dad and I live with my dog, Sindbad, in Evanston, Illinois. If you saw Sindbad you might

laugh. He's a miniature dachshund, with a long skinny body, very short legs, and big floppy ears that fly out like wings when he runs. Most cats are bigger than Sindbad, but Mom says you shouldn't let his small size fool you because he's also stubborn, courageous, and loyal.

I want to be a veterinarian when I grow up, and as you might guess, I love all sorts of animals. Even bugs and worms. I like to pretend I'm a scientist, and so I'm always on the lookout for interesting specimens. Once I found a caterpillar on a carrot plant in our garden. I put it in my bug jar and fed it carrot leaves until it spun a green chrysalis. One day, after what seemed like forever, I saw that a beautiful butterfly—a black swallowtail butterfly—

had come out of the chrysalis. I shouted to my mom, and we both stood there amazed, watching it slowly flap its big blue and black wings. She was as excited as I was and, just like me, kept saying, "I don't believe it! I don't believe it!"

I don't know about you, but schedules aren't my favorite thing, and so I love summer more than any other time of the year. Some of my best summer days are when I can persuade my mom to finish work early and take me and a friend swimming at Lighthouse Beach. The beach is just a few miles from our house, and there really is a lighthouse. Lake Michigan is so HUGE that it has beaches in three other states besides Illinois! When I was really little I thought it was an ocean.

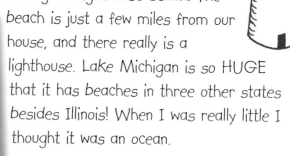

I love the lake when it's as smooth and bright as a mirror, and I also love it when the waves are so big that you can bodysurf in them. Sometimes we actually swim (especially my mom, who likes to do laps like she's in a pool), but mostly we just play games like tag in the water and build sand castles. Coming home Mom always says, "Boy did that feel good!" and I always say, "I knew you'd like it! Let's go again tomorrow, OK?"

Other Favorite Summer Things

catching fireflies in the backyard

 playing with my friends
and with Sindbad at Porter Park

running outside when there's a storm
to feel the wind and rain

drawing
dragons

and
fish

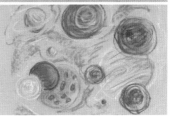

and
planets
with chalk on the sidewalk

reading in my special cozy chair next to
Dad's dusty, old, wooden desk

9

Mom has her own summer routines.
Putting away our winter clothes and bringing
out summer shorts and dresses. Pulling weeds and helping
Dad clean up the screen porch. And going to
her doctor's office for her yearly physical
check-up. My mom never makes a fuss
about those things, so I normally don't pay
much attention to them. This year was
different, though. This year she got a call
from her doctor a few days after she had
her check-up. He told her that she might have a tumor in one
of her breasts. A tumor is a lump that is growing in the body.

Clover

WEED

It's a lump that shouldn't be there.

Ring uauuuuuuuuuuummmmmmmm

At first Mom didn't tell me that she might have a tumor, but
I could tell that my parents were worried about something.
They were spending a lot of time on the phone talking in
serious voices, and forgot to remind me to practice the piano.
I told myself that nothing was wrong,
but deep inside I started to have a bad
feeling that this wasn't going to be
a regular summer.

Ring Ring
Ring Ring
Ring
Ring
Ring
Ring

10

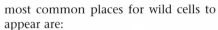

When Cells Go Wild

Doctors recommend that adults visit their doctor about once a year for a physical check-up. During the visit, the doctor makes sure that everything is healthy by looking at, listening to, and feeling the body. The doctor also uses x-rays and other tests to see what his or her eyes can't.

In the same way that x-rays help doctors find a broken bone or help dentists find hidden cavities in teeth, x-ray pictures of other parts of the body help doctors check for cells that are unhealthy.

A cell is the smallest living part of the body. Different parts of your body are made up of different kinds of cells. For example, skin cells cover your body from head to toe, your bones are made of bone cells, and blood cells circulate through your body. The stomach is formed of cells that digest food, the cells of the lung take in oxygen, and a woman's breast has special cells that can make milk.

Our bodies can make new cells, which is very important because some cells grow old and need to be replaced with fresh ones. In fact, our bodies are always changing, becoming new again, from the minute that we are born.

Very rarely, though, our bodies make new cells that don't obey the rules. These "wild cells" keep making new cells when new cells aren't needed. An x-ray can find signs of wild cells in a person's body. X-rays can reveal wild cells in many different parts of the body. The most common places for wild cells to appear are:

- the skin,
- the lung,
- the large intestine
  (also called the colon),
- the prostate
  (a very small organ that is only in males, located near the bladder),
- the breast.

An x-ray of the breast is called a mammogram. Many women have mammograms during their regular check-ups. Having a mammogram is like checking your tent for rattlesnakes or bears when you're camping. Almost always, a mammogram shows that no wild cells are present. But it's a good idea for women to have regular breast checkups just to be sure.

X-ray pictures may not look like much to most people, but to a

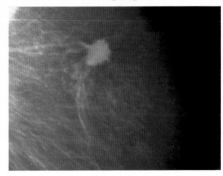

radiologist—a doctor who specializes in looking at x-ray pictures—they tell a lot. Do you see the pink spot in this false-color x-ray picture? It is a group of cells that are not growing in a normal way. When cells start growing in a crazy, disorganized way, they can form a lump called a tumor.

When a group of cells grow out of control, they can begin to crowd out healthy cells and form a lump called a malignant tumor. Malignant means cancerous. Luckily, most tumors are not malignant.

Red Blood Cells

Lung Cells

Bone-forming Cells

JULY

For a while my parents kept acting like everything was normal. On the 4th of July, we all walked up to Central Street to watch the parade. My mom and dad and I love that parade, even though it's the same every year with the usual marching bands, clowns, tumblers, the mayor, and kids riding their bikes.

Later, we went to my best friend Jamie's house for a picnic, and of course, we all went to watch the fireworks when it got dark.

Usually Mom loves the fireworks. She always says they remind her of enormous chrysanthemums. But she wasn't paying much attention this year. Now I understand why. She was probably thinking about the little operation that she was about to have, called a biopsy. The biopsy would tell my mom if she had a malignant tumor.

WHAT IS A BIOPSY?

During a biopsy, a doctor removes part or all of a lump. Then another doctor, who specializes in looking at cells under a microscope to see if they are unhealthy, checks the cells from the lump. It is this doctor—called a pathologist—who figures out whether a tumor is malignant or harmless.

My mom's tumor did turn out to be malignant. After the doctor told her that, she finally explained to me what was happening. She told me what a tumor is, and how she would be having an operation to make sure that all of the tumor was removed.

I sure was glad my parents told me about the tumor because I could tell that something was going on, and now at least I knew what it was. Mom reassured me that she would be fine, but still I didn't like it that she had to stay overnight in the hospital. The thought that she wouldn't be coming right home after her operation made my stomach feel tight and fluttery. I kept thinking,

My MOM in the HOSPITAL?!

When I went to visit Mom in the hospital after her operation, I wasn't expecting her to look so pale and weak. I felt sad and afraid when I first saw her—
like that wasn't really my mom lying there,
with a tube in her nose and
another tube connected to her hand. Some scary thoughts started to buzz in my head, like,

"Will my mom be all right?"

"Who will take care of me if she doesn't get better?"

14

Surgery

One of the main ways that doctors treat cancer is with surgery—by delicately cutting a tumor from a person's body, using either a special knife or a laser. A laser is a device that sends out a very narrow and powerful beam of light. Doctors surgically remove tumors from many parts of the body, including the bone, the lung, the liver, the brain, the breast, the bladder, and the large intestine.

If a tumor is small, doctors may need to remove only part of the affected organ, bone, or other body part. For example, when a person has bladder cancer, doctors can often simply scrape or burn away the malignant cells. Similarly, when someone has cancer in the large intestine (colon cancer), doctors can often remove the part of the intestine with the tumor, and then reconnect the healthy parts of the intestine. When a woman has breast cancer, doctors often remove only the area of the breast where the lump is, an operation called a lumpectomy (lump-ectomy). *Ectomy* comes from the Greek word for "cut."

When a tumor is large, or when there are many small tumors, doctors are likely to remove most or all of the affected body part, if it is one that we can get along without. There are many parts of the body that we don't need in order to stay healthy, including the bladder, the kidneys, the breasts, the large intestine, the stomach, the uterus, the ovaries, and certain bones. Either the body can still do all of its necessary jobs without the body part, or doctors have ways to help the body do the jobs that the missing part usually handles.

For example, the body manages fine without certain reproductive organs, such as the uterus or breasts. When a woman's uterus is removed, she can no longer give birth, but her body remains as healthy as it ever was. Similarly, a woman can get along very well without breasts because she can use milk from a different source to feed her baby. When doctors remove most or all of a woman's breast—an operation called a mastectomy, which comes from the Greek word for "breast" *(mastos)*— she may have another operation in which doctors create a new breast. The new breast looks much like the old one, but it cannot make milk.

We have several organs that can be safely removed even though they do jobs that are necessary for the body's health. When the bladder is entirely removed, for example, or when the healthy parts of the large intestine cannot be reconnected, doctors can create another way for urine and solid waste to leave the body.

Just as we have two feet, two hands, and two ears, some of our organs also come in pairs. The body usually only needs one of these two organs to function. For example, we have two kidneys, so if one is removed, the remaining kidney simply does the work of both. The same is true for lungs and ovaries: one is all the body really needs to get along. If both kidneys need to be removed, a special machine can do the kidneys' job of cleaning a person's blood and making urine.

Another option that doctors have is the use of medicines to help the body function when certain parts have been removed. For example, the body has organs called glands that make hormones. Hormones are special chemicals that the body needs in order to work right. The thyroid and the pancreas are two examples of glands that produce essential hormones. Scientists have created medicines that contain these same chemicals, so that people who have had these organs surgically removed can still get the hormones they need.

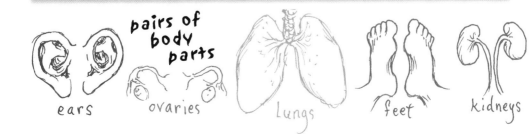

pairs of body parts

ears   ovaries   lungs   feet   kidneys

Dad noticed that I was upset. He started to show me how the thin plastic tube in Mom's nose went to an oxygen tank. He explained that all of the cells in our body need oxygen, so the extra oxygen that Mom was breathing through the tube was helping her body recover more quickly.

He also said that the other tube, the one in her hand, was helping her recover more quickly by giving her body extra fluids. The cells in her body could get the water and minerals they needed much faster this way than if she drank the same amount.

The doctor who operated on my mom stopped by to check on her, and Dad introduced me to him. His name was Dr. Winchester. I shook his hand. He was calm and nice and he seemed smart. I liked him. I remember thinking, "My mom has a really good doctor and he'll know how to make her better."

Can you imagine being afraid to hug or kiss your mom or dad because of cancer? I knew that you can't catch

cancer, but still I wasn't sure that
I should kiss my mom goodbye.
I thought she might be too sensitive
or sickly. Most of all, she just
looked so different, and that
scared me. But then she hugged
and kissed me, and asked me a lot of questions about what
I'd been doing. I think it was then that the fluttery feeling in
my stomach started to get better. I thought to myself,
"She's going to be OK."

When it was time to go
I gave my mom a get-well
card that I had made for
her, and she gave me a big
smile and another kiss.
When Dad and I were going
out the door, I saw Mom
reading my card again. It
made me feel good inside
to know that she would be
looking at that card and
thinking of me, just like I
would be thinking of her
when I saw her stuff lying
round the house.

17

We brought Mom home from the hospital after a few days. I helped out by carrying her overnight bag. It takes a while for a person's appetite to come back after an operation, so Mom didn't feel like eating much of the celebration lunch that Dad and I had cooked.

Welcome Home
Lunch

tomato soup

tuna salad
on whole wheat bread

carrot sticks

brownies

I told her, "That's OK, I understand," so that she wouldn't feel bad, but really I felt like crying. I think I felt all mixed up inside. I was relieved the operation was over, and I was definitely happy to have Mom home. But I wanted her to make my lunch, and take me to the library, and do all the other things that she usually did for me. I guess I really wanted my mom to be the same as before so that I would know that she was completely OK.

There was something else, too. Something I barely knew how to put into words. I don't think I really WANTED to put it into words, because whenever I started to think about this THING I felt terrible. It was a nagging question that made me feel like hiding away from everyone, even my friends.

Here it is:

How did my Mom get CANCER? Could I have done something to make her get sick??????

I worried about it for a long time. I was afraid to ask until a lot later, though, because I was afraid of what the answer might be.

AUGUST

August was sort of a boring month at our house. Mom did a lot of resting. And a lot of talking with my grandma and aunt who had come to visit. I felt a little like wallpaper. Oh, everybody was nice to me. They just weren't paying much attention to me. Sometimes I would watch TV for hours—which I'd never been allowed to do before—and nobody said a word. I felt like I could walk on the ceiling and nobody would even notice! This might not have been so bad except I also felt angry and impatient, which made me feel really awful because it seemed so selfish.

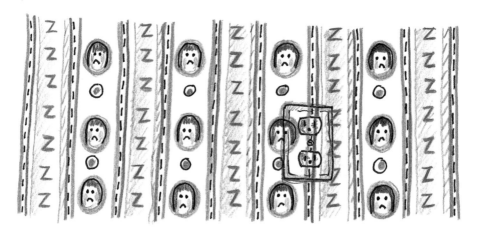

Luckily Sindbad knew how I was feeling. I can tell him anything, and he never gets upset. He just jumps onto my lap with this concerned look on his face, listens to every word I tell him, and licks me all over my face to make me feel better. After talking to Sindbad I would feel a lot calmer. I could even remember some of the things my dad had told me about hanging in there, and being patient. "Things will get better," he said, "you just have to give them time."

For a couple of weeks, my mom had a plastic tube attached just below her armpit to help her heal from the operation. I couldn't believe that she never complained about that tube, which looked like this:

N E W S B R I E F

Drainage Tubes

Doctors have been using drainage tubes to help wounds heal after surgery for more than 100 years. Our bodies have a clear liquid, called lymph, that circulates throughout the body, just as blood does. Lymph is very important for helping wounds heal, because it carries nourishment (food) to all the tissues in the body and cleans away waste. However, if too much lymph collects in one place, then the lymph can't move freely and do its nourishing and cleaning jobs. The healing process slows down, or a wound can even become infected.

When a tumor or organ has been surgically removed, a drainage tube helps keep lymph from collecting in the area. Any excess lymph drains out through the tube and into a little plastic pouch attached to the bottom end of the tube. The tube usually stays in place for about two weeks, until the plastic pouch shows that a normal amount of lymph is draining from the area of the surgery. The drainage tube is taken out by a nurse—its removal usually does not hurt and is very simple, taking less than a minute.

No More Tubes!

Mom knew that the tube was just temporary, but still it felt weird and a little uncomfortable, so she was very happy when she didn't need it anymore and it was taken out.

I think it was after the tube came out that my mom started smiling again. That was a big relief, because our neighbor who lives across the street, Mrs. Carpenter, couldn't stop crying when she had cancer.

determined

Sad

Worried

Spiritual

calm

Angry

fearful

I know that because every time Mom and I saw her she would start to cry. And then there was my friend Jamie's uncle, who became very sad and quiet and didn't want to see people when he had cancer. I asked Mom why she wasn't crying like Mrs. Carpenter.

"Everyone's different," she said. "Having cancer is hard for everybody, but people react a lot of different ways." I told her I was really glad she didn't seem so sad. She said, "I cry, too, sometimes. But mostly I try to forget about being sick by thinking about what I can do to get better. That's why I'm working so hard on my arm exercises." When she said that, I wished I could give her something beautiful, like a big bouquet of flowers. "Love you, Mom," I whispered in her ear.

You're probably wondering why my mom needed to do arm exercises. When she first came back from the hospital, she couldn't raise her arm above her waist.

Not because the muscles in her arm were weak, but because the operation had made the muscles in her shoulder and under her arm so tight. She needed to stretch them out gradually by doing the exercises every day, several times a day.

Mom said that lots of people who have surgery for cancer need to do special exercises to help their muscles work the way they used to. She said that there are even special exercises for people who need to learn how to walk again after they've had a tumor removed from their leg.

Mom had a videotape from the hospital that showed her how to do her arm exercises. I got pretty sick of that tape, especially when I had a video that I wanted to watch! I guess all of Mom's hard work was worth it, though, because by the end of August she was able to move her arm in all the ways that she could before her operation.

SEPTEMBER

In September, when I went back to school, things were almost the same as the year before because I was with the same group of kids. My teacher was Mrs. Kaplan. Mrs. Kaplan is not only a really good teacher, she's one of my favorite people. She never minded if I hung around the classroom at the end of the school day so that I could have her all to myself for a few minutes before I ran for my bus. I would usually race for the bus just as the doors were closing,

but it was definitely always worth it. If I were president, there would be a special award for teachers who help kids feel better when they're going through hard times!

But like I said, not everything about school was normal. Sometimes I had

Mrs. Kaplan

to eat hot lunch instead of my usual salami sandwich, because Dad forgot to make my lunch. Or I had to wear jeans that were too small because my parents got behind in the wash. Here's my list of things that guarantee a lousy school day:

Top 5 Things that Guarantee
☹ A LOUSY DAY

5. BAD WEATHER MEANS EVERYONE STAYS INSIDE DURING LUNCH AND RECESS.

4. A TOILET OVERFLOWS IN THE SCHOOL BATHROOM AGAIN YUCK!!!

3. I GET STUCK NEXT TO TOBY the BULLY IN GYM.

2. I LOSE MY READING REPORT FOR THE 2ND WEEK IN A ROW AND GET A BAD GRADE AND A LECTURE.

1. (THE WORST THING) I HAVE NOTHING TO WEAR EXCEPT JEANS THAT DON'T EVEN REACH MY SOCKS, AND HAVE TO SPEND THE DAY LISTENING TO MY SO-CALLED FRIENDS AND EVERYONE ELSE MAKING REALLY CLEVER REMARKS LIKE "Hey, NICE PANTS!"

The thing that bothered me the most, though, was that my mom didn't drive me to school in the mornings. Instead, I had to go to our neighbors the Jacksons, and ride with them. Dad explained that it was good for Mom to be able to sleep later in the morning. But I still wished that I could ride with Mom, even though we usually rushed around and shouted things at each other like, "Wait! I forgot my lunch!" and "You're going to make me late for my train!"

One day, when I was completely fed up with everything and had to blow off some steam, I yelled,

I feel like a shirt stuffed in a suitcase in that car!

Like a backpack crammed into a locker!

I'm a pickle in a sandwich, squashed between two slices of bread named Vanessa and Brandon!

Mom looked at me for a l-o-n-g second, and then we both started to laugh. When we stopped laughing she asked me why I didn't like riding with the Jacksons to school. "It makes me feel like a baby," I said. "Like our family is helpless. And besides, I like riding to school with you, so that we can talk."

Mom rubbed my back the way I love and said something really nice. She said, "I miss those times, too. Just remember, it won't be forever. Do you think you can handle it for another couple of months?" I felt a lot better knowing that she liked our hurry-up-or-we'll-be-late drive in the morning as much as I did. And I liked figuring out what was really bothering me— that felt good, too. But I also felt kind of silly for giving my mom such a hard time about it. "I guess so, Mom," I said in a pretend cranky voice and rolled my eyes, and we both laughed a little more.

Later that day I thought to myself, "Wait a minute. I'm not old enough to drive myself to school, but I CAN wash my own clothes and make my own lunch!" The more I thought about it, the more I wanted to do those things, so I made a plan and wrote it down. Here it is (don't pay any attention to the smudgy parts...they're from Sindbad walking across my paper):

MY PLAN

1. I Will learn to use the washing machine and dryer and **WASH MY OWN CLOTHES!**

(well, maybe NOT ALL of my clothes — but at least the 👕 T-shirts + jeans 👖 I wear a lot.) 🧦🧦

REMINDER: Don't WASTE WATER!

*If you don't have enough of your own dirty clothes to make a full load, add some of Mom's and Dad's.

2. I Will pack my **OWN LUNCH** 🎒 — the 🌙 Night before, so that I'm not late for SCHOOL!

Dad ↓

(that way, Dad can relax and enjoy his breakfast — and I'll be able to make sure there aren't any WEIRD or MYSTERIOUS foods in my lunches. NO MORE ~~TUNA~~ SARDINES 🐟 (DISGUSTING)!!! at least NOT in the sandwiches that I bring from home!

JUICE OR MILK

PB + 🍯

I talked to Mom and Dad, and they really liked my plan. I learned to do those things, and some others too. My mom says she doesn't know anyone who can sort and fold clean clothes as quickly as I can. So that's my job now. My other specialty? Making toast and eggs for Sunday morning breakfast!

The big event for my mom in September was that she started chemotherapy. Chemotherapy is a very strong medicine that kills cancer cells.

I didn't understand why Mom had to have more treatment. She explained that doctors give a person chemotherapy after surgery if they think there's any chance that some malignant cells might have traveled from the place where the tumor was to some other part of the body.

Mom also said that the chemotherapy treatments would make her hair fall out. "You mean you'll be bald?" I asked. When she said that she would be bald but that her hair would grow back, I only heard the bald part. I thought of her lying there in the hospital after her surgery and started to feel scared again. Would she look weird without any hair?

I tried to be cool, though, and think of something funny to say. What came out was: "Nobody remembers what they looked like when they were babies, so I think it will be very interesting for you to see what you looked like when you were a bald baby."

I think my mom knew I was scared anyway, because she gave me a hug and said, "Don't worry. My hair will be back before you know it!"

When my mom's hair fell out, she didn't look that different because she wore hats. Here are some of the different kinds of hats she wore:

Chemotherapy

Chemotherapy is the use of strong medicines to kill cancer cells. Sometimes the medicine is injected directly into the area of the body where there was or still is a tumor. Other times doctors want the cancer-fighting medicine to flow through a person's bloodstream to nearly every part of the body.

When chemotherapy medicines go throughout a person's entire body, some healthy cells can get destroyed along with the unhealthy ones. Chemotherapy medicines target fast-growing cells. Malignant cells are fast-growing, but so are certain other cells, such as hair cells and the cells deep inside bones that make blood cells. These can also be destroyed by anti-cancer medicines, which is why many people look pale and feel tired after their chemotherapy treatments and why they sometimes lose their hair.

Chemotherapy is like a powerful giant that can clear a field of harmful weeds but can't help stepping on a few flowers along the way. Some flowers, though, no matter how much they're stepped on, keep coming back. Hair is like that: as soon as chemotherapy is finished, hair starts to grow back again.

When people are being treated with cancer-fighting drugs, they are carefully watched over by a doctor who specializes in giving chemotherapy. Usually, people go to the hospital or to their doctor's office when they are getting their chemotherapy treatments.

Chemotherapy can be given in several ways: by injection, by mouth in the form of pills or liquid medicine, and intravenously, which means "in a vein." (A vein is a type of blood vessel.) Chemotherapy medicines given by mouth and intravenously circulate through the entire body in the bloodstream. When given intravenously, the medicine drips from a plastic bag, down a thin tube, and through a needle that has been inserted into a blood vessel in the arm or leg. It takes about two hours for all of the medicine to drip into the bloodstream.

A person with cancer will receive several chemotherapy treatments, each a few weeks after the one before. For example, women with breast cancer are usually given chemotherapy every few weeks for four to six months. Other forms of cancer may require chemotherapy for as long as a year.

The number of chemotherapy treatments depends on several things: the kind of cancer and tumor a person has, how large the tumor is, where the tumor is located in the body, and whether malignant cells from the tumor are growing in other parts of the body. The number of chemotherapy treatments also depends on a person's age and general health. For example, the number of chemotherapy treatments is often different for children and adults, even when their tumors are very similar. The doctor creates a treatment plan to fit each person's particular needs.

POWERFUL GIANT

She even wore a hat to
bed, to keep her head warm!

One day, when Mom first started wearing hats, she asked me
if I wanted to put some of her hair outside for the birds to
use when building their nests,
like we do after I get
a haircut. Birds love
hair and dryer lint
and pet fur and just
about anything else
soft that makes a
nice bed. It's so cool
to think that baby birds
are hatching on my hair
clippings or on bits of fuzz
from my clothes!

Anyway, I said "sure!" but instead of sprinkling it in the
back yard, I secretly put it in a box. Later, when Mom
found the box, she asked me why I had kept
her hair. I didn't know exactly—I just
knew that I wanted to keep
it. I felt better knowing that
it was someplace safe.

I kept that hair for a pretty long time—until Mom's hair started to grow back and I had a dream about birds and eggs and nests. When I woke up from the dream, I pulled the box out from under the bed, opened it, and looked at all the handfuls of hair. "I don't need to keep this anymore," I thought.

We need a softer nest!

"IT'S JUST HAIR."

It was freezing cold outside, but I opened my window, leaned out as far as I could, and sprinkled some of the hair on the white snow below. "This is for you, birdies," I said. Then I tipped over the box, and the rest of the hair floated gently down to the ground.

34

About the same time that I hid Mom's hair in a box, Dad went away on a business trip. Just Mom and I were at home. When we were alone together it was harder for me to forget about her cancer. Also, that horrible feeling I didn't want to think about—that I might have done something to make my mom sick—got stronger and stronger.

One night after dinner I was sitting on the floor, gluing pictures into my scrapbook, while Mom was lying down and reading on the couch. In my stack were some photos I had taken on the 4th of July. When I saw them, I thought about how much things had changed since that day.

"When will your hair grow *back?*" I asked her. "Mmm, in about three months," she said from the other side of her book. "Does that seem like a really long time?" "Not really," I said, and went back to sorting and gluing pictures.

Sneaking a look at my mom, I thought how good it felt to be near her. And then the words just came blurting out of my mouth: "Did I do anything that made you get cancer, Mom?" It was like a monster leaping out of a closet. It didn't even feel like it was me doing the talking!

Mom looked around her book at me for a minute with this funny face that was surprised and loving and even a little worried all at the same time. "Oh, Clare, of course you didn't," she said. "Cancer is definitely not caused by anything that another person says or does." Then she sat up and told me that the cell changes that caused her tumor to start growing might have even happened before I was born! When Mom said that, something tight and heavy inside me went away. I felt like laughing and dancing. Before I went to bed that night I did do a little dance, just for myself and Sindbad and the bright full moon outside my window.

36

I've always looked forward to Halloween. I love dressing up and going trick-or-treating.

Usually Mom and I would make my costume together, and I would have lots of different ideas for it. Last year I was the Statue of Liberty. (I used a cardboard egg carton to make my crown.) Other years I've been a monarch butterfly, Robin Hood, and a mermaid.

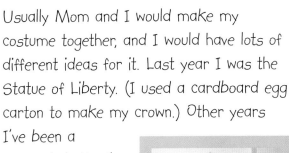

37

This year, though, Mom didn't have the energy to work on my costume, and instead of feeling excited about Halloween I felt a little sad. I had a hard time thinking of something I could be.

And then my dad came up with a great idea: I could be a treasure map! How do you do that, you might be wondering? Well, here's a picture of me in my costume:

It's funny. After I made my Halloween costume, I started doing a bunch of things that I hadn't done for a while, and even some new things. Instead of watching television all the time, I started taking Sindbad for a run around the block, and shooting hoops with my friends in Porter Pork. I played board games with Mom and Dad, and started this journal. I went to the library a lot, so that I could find out more about things like tumors and chemotherapy, and I even made copies of information from good books to put in my journal. Best of all, though, my friend Jamie and I took a judo class together. That was really fun.

NOVEMBER

In the middle of November things started to get back to normal. Mom finished her chemotherapy and went back to work. I didn't realize how much I missed hearing the getting-ready-for-work noises Mom made in the morning. The first time I woke up and got dressed to the sound of her taking a shower I felt like cheering. Best of all was the sound of her shouting,

"Hustle up, Clare, or we'll be late!"

It was in November that my mom started her last kind of treatment—radiation therapy. Radiation therapy is when doctors use strong x-rays or other invisible rays to destroy cancer cells.

DECEMBER

When Mom was having her radiation treatments she seemed to talk a lot less than usual. She read a lot of mystery novels, and went to sleep way before my dad and I did. It was like she was hibernating, like a bear in her cave in the winter. She seemed kind of far away, even though she was right in the house.

The good part about this time was that my dad and I got extra close. Usually Mom made sure that I did my homework and that I brushed my teeth. Now Dad did those things. If I had a bad day at school, I would tell him about it while we did the dishes. He would listen and help me think of what to do or say to make things better. Even though Dad and I missed Mom, it was a nice time—peaceful, sort of like the snowfall outside.

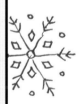

Radiation

Radiation therapy is the use of high-energy rays from x-rays or other sources to destroy cancer cells. Doctors use radiation therapy to destroy a malignant tumor that can't be cut out, or to shrink a tumor before it is removed, or to kill any cancer cells that might remain in a person's body after a tumor has been removed.

Usually a person gets radiation therapy from a large machine that aims high-powered x-rays at the area of the body where there was or still is a tumor. For example, if a person has lung cancer, the x-rays are pointed at the area of the lung where there is or was a tumor. If a woman has had a lumpectomy, the high-powered rays are aimed at the part of her breast where the tumor used to be. (Radiation therapy is less often given to women who have had a mastectomy.) The x-rays used in radiation therapy are much, much more powerful than those used to check for a break in a bone or for cavities in teeth.

When a person receives radiation from a machine, each treatment lasts a few minutes. Usually the treatments are given five days a week for several weeks. Sometimes the skin on the part of the body being treated becomes itchy and dry, or red and sore as if sunburned. Receiving radiation therapy can also make a person feel tired. These problems quickly go away once the treatments are finished.

Because the high-powered x-rays in radiation therapy can also hurt healthy cells, a doctor who specializes in giving radiation is very careful when setting up the machine. This doctor makes sure that the right amount of x-rays is given, and that the x-rays go only to the area of the patient's body where they are needed.

There is another way to get radiation therapy. Doctors can also put a small container filled with radioactive material directly on a tumor. This is called a "radiation implant." Sometimes a radiation implant is left inside the person's body for a short time, and sometimes it is left inside permanently.

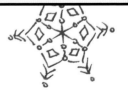

New Year

Toward the end of December my mom's hair started to grow back. I would see her stroking her head, and I liked to touch it, too. The new hair felt so soft and silky, just like the fur on a kitten. On New Year's Eve we all got dressed up and went to a big party. Here's a picture of Mom at the party with her new hair and NO HAT!

Mom had her last radiation treatment on January 2nd. After that, she got better fast. Her energy came back—LOTS of energy. She started exercising a lot, and she took a portrait drawing class. She made some really cool drawings of me, and let me use her charcoal sticks so that I could make some portraits of her. Here's one of my drawings we put up on the fridge.

She went on an organizing spree, tidying closets all around the house, and made me clean my room really well. I grumbled and argued the whole time,

BEFORE
What a mess!

AFTER
So organized!

but really that was just out of habit. Secretly I enjoyed the hustle and bustle, and that feeling of a fresh start you get when your room is newly clean. Best of all, though, was seeing Mom be her old self again!

During spring vacation, Dad and Mom and I went on a trip, our first in almost a year. We went to Tucson, Arizona, and walked in the mountains there. We saw wildflowers blooming in the desert and a whole forest of huge Saguaro cacti.

(I always thought the plural for cactus was cactuses...but it's cacti! Isn't that a cool word?)

One day, we hiked up a steep, winding trail that seemed to go on forever. Near the top of the mountain we all stopped to rest and to look way, way down to the bottom of the trail where we started. I can still remember how happy I felt while we sat there looking at the yellow and red desert flowers and the thousands of cacti spread out like a blanket in the little canyon below us.

I LOVE DRAWING SAGUARO CACTI !!!!!

44

I shut my eyes and leaned against my mom, and thought about all that happened since last year and how sometimes I felt like there wasn't room in my head to think about anything else. "Do you ever wish this year had never happened, Mom?" I asked.

She thought for a minute. Then she said, "Well, getting cancer isn't something I would have asked for, but I think there are some really good things that came out of it." I knew she was saying something important, but what did she mean? Good things from cancer? "Like what?" I asked her.

"Well," she said, "like this conversation we're having right now. I'm not sure we would have been comfortable talking like this a year ago. After I got sick, there were some pretty tough things we had to talk about, and it wasn't easy. Still, we did it, and I think that's made us grow closer as a family."

45

That got us all talking, and we came up with a whole bunch of other good things:

Because of Mom's cancer we all had to go through a lot of changes, and that has made us stronger. (Like when I learned to do my own laundry and make my own lunch.)

We learned to help each other in new ways, and to appreciate each other's courage and kindness.

We found out how caring and helpful people are. (Dad said he didn't mean just the doctors and nurses, but people from school and work, and all our friends and family.)

The cancer reminded us of how much we love each other.

We stuck together and encouraged each other.

 We kept doing the things we love: playing, and working, and making jokes.

46

I remember how the conversation ended. Dad told us something really cool. He said, "I know now that our family can handle just about anything." When he said that, I felt very proud, like I'd been given some kind of medal. Do you know what popped into my mind then?

A picture of me climbing a tree, and then hanging by my knees from a tree branch, and then bouncing up and down on the branch, knowing that it would never, ever break. That's when I started to smile, a smile that just kept getting bigger and bigger until I thought I'd burst.

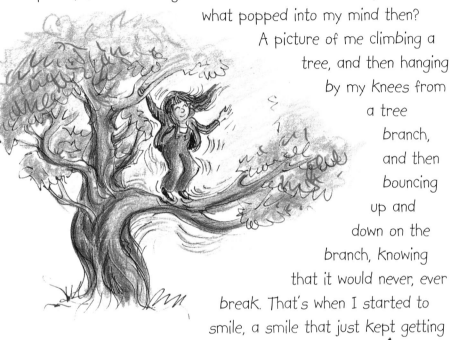

"You're the best," I said, jumping up.

And then we raced to the top of the ridge and waved our caps in the air.

May

Mom had her birthday in May, and a mammogram to make sure that everything was normal. When the radiologist told her that her mammogram was fine, she said she felt like she'd been given the best birthday present ever.

By then her hair had grown back thick and curly! (Mom said it was the chemotherapy that caused her hair to grow back curly, and that it would probably stay curly for about a year.)

Sometimes, when I look at my mom's new, short hair, I think about how much I've changed too. I used to think that things would always stay pretty much the same. Now I know that things can change really fast. I see now that things can't always be the way I want them to be, but I'm happy anyway. Why is that? Maybe because I discovered that a lot of things I was most afraid of didn't turn out to be so bad after all. Also, I found out that I can handle a lot more than I thought I could, and that feels pretty good.

The year my mother was bald is definitely one I'll never forget. But right now I'm thinking about how summer is almost here, and how I'm going to sleep late, swim every day if I can, and learn to ride a unicycle. Any day now Mom will start pulling weeds and cleaning up the screen porch. And who knows, maybe I'll find a whole family of black swallowtail butterflies in the garden. It's going to be a great summer!

RESOURCES

FREE BOOKLETS

Children with Cancer in the Family: Dealing with Diagnosis
Provides information on how to tell children about a cancer
diagnosis. For a free copy of this essay, published by the
American Cancer Society, call 800-ACS-2345. **Note:** The
following two related items, also published by the American
Cancer Society, can be ordered as companion pieces.

Children with Cancer in the Family: Dealing with Treatment
A short but highly informative guide for parents that answers
such questions as:
- What kind of information do children need about a parent's
  treatment?
- How do families deal with the uncertainty of not knowing if
  a parent's treatment has been successful?
- Are there special issues for teenagers in dealing with a
  parent's cancer?

For a free copy, contact the American Cancer Society
at 800-ACS-2345.

Children with Cancer in the Family: Understanding Psychosocial Support Services

Published by the American Cancer Society, this essay addresses common psychological and social issues that families may face when a parent or grandparent has cancer. Specific information is provided to assist the parent with helping the young or adolescent child. To order, call 800-ACS-2345.

Closing In on Cancer: Solving a 5000-Year-Old Mystery (NIH Publication No. 98-2955)

This free booklet, published by the National Cancer Institute, was not written for children, but it has many pictures and a great deal of fascinating information in an accessible format. To order, call 800-4-CANCER (800-422-6237).

It Helps to Have Friends When Mom or Dad Has Cancer

Free booklet published by the American Cancer Society. To order call 800-ACS-2345.

Kids Worry Too

Helps parents recognize some of the reactions and concerns children may have when a family member is hospitalized, and provides suggestions for helping them cope. This booklet is published by the Child Life Department, Nebraska Health System, 982165 Nebraska Medical Center, Omaha, NE 68198-2165. A copy can be ordered by calling 402-559-6775.

Someone I Love Has Cancer

This booklet for younger children includes many drawing
activities for understanding feelings as well as basic
information about cancer and its treatment. It is published by
the Minnesota Division of the American Cancer Society and
can be ordered for free by calling 800-582-5152 or by writing
to the American Cancer Society, Minnesota Division, Inc.,
3316 West 66th Street, Minneapolis, MN 55435.

What About Me? A Booklet for Teenage Children
of Cancer Patients
(By Linda Leopold Strauss, copyright 1986)
This booklet is published by Cancer Family Care,
7182 Reading Road, Suite 1201, Cincinnati, OH 45237,
and can be ordered by calling 513-731-3346.

When Someone in Your Family Has Cancer
(NIH Publication No. 96-2685)
This free booklet, written for children, is published by the
National Cancer Institute and can be ordered by calling
800-4-CANCER (800-422-6237).

Organizations and Online Sites

American Cancer Society (ACS) (national headquarters)

1599 Clifton Rd., NE

Atlanta, GA 30329

Phone: 404-320-3333

Toll-free phone: 800-ACS-2345

Web site: www.cancer.org

The American Cancer Society is a voluntary organization with local branches throughout the country. The ACS supports cancer research, conducts educational programs, and offers many free support services to patients and their families, including the Reach to Recovery program for breast cancer patients, transportation to and from treatment, and "tic" (a catalog offering special products such as wigs, hats, and breast prostheses).

The ACS also offers a wide array of informational materials, books for parents and for children, and an online community for survivors and caregivers. For free booklets, or to obtain information about local programs, books, and services, call 800-ACS-2345 or visit online at www.cancer.org. You can also find the telephone number for your local ACS branch in the white pages of the telephone book.

You can speak with a trained cancer information specialist or a nurse at no charge by calling the American Cancer Society's hotline at 800-ACS-2345. Calling this toll-free number will connect you to the National Cancer Information Center in Austin, Texas, which employs 154 cancer information specialists and six oncology nurses to answer cancer-related questions. Phones are staffed 24 hours a day, seven days a week.

American Institute for Cancer Research (AICR)
1759 R St., NW
Washington, DC 20003
Toll-free phone: 800-843-8114 (202-328-7744 in DC)
Web site: www.aicr.org

The American Institute for Cancer Research focuses exclusively on the link between diet and cancer. It provides a wide range of education programs, information, and booklets that help individuals learn to make dietary changes for lower cancer risk. To order free brochures, or to print copies of articles and recipes online, go to the Institute's Web site at www.aicr.org.

Canadian Cancer Society (national headquarters)

10 Alcorn Ave., Suite 200

Toronto, Ontario

Canada M4V 3B1

Phone: 416-961-7223

Fax: 416-961-4189

The Canadian Cancer Society offers many of the same services as the American Cancer Society.

Cancer Care, Inc. (national office)

275 7th Ave.

New York, NY 10001

Phone: 212-302-2400

Toll-free phone: 800-813-HOPE (4673)

Fax: 212-719-0263

Web site: www.cancercare.org

A national, nonprofit organization that helps people with cancer, their families, and caregivers. Cancer Care's services, which are free of charge, include information, one-to-one counseling, specialized support groups, educational programs, telephone contact, and a Web site. Call their toll-free number or visit them online.

CaringKids

An Internet-wide e-mail discussion group for children who know someone who is ill. Grownups are not permitted to participate on this list, as its purpose is to provide children with their own safe place to share. Automatic subscription is available at Oncolink's Web site.
Go to: http://www.oncolink.com/templates/coping/
article.cfm?c=6&s=29&ss=65&id=455

Kid Support, Inc.

2607 Simpson Street
Evanston, IL 60201-2134
Phone: 847-869-7743
Web site: www.kid-support.org

Kid Support, a nonprofit, charitable organization dedicated to helping children cope when a parent has cancer, offers training and curriculum for establishing adult-led peer support groups that provide children with age-appropriate information about cancer, promote children's discussion about what they are feeling and thinking, teach children coping skills, and enhance family communication about cancer.

Kids Konnected

27071 Cabot Rd., Suite 102

Laguna Hills, CA 92653

Toll-free phone: 800-899-2866

Fax: 949-582-3983

Web site: www.kidskonnected.org

Kids Konnected is a national nonprofit organization that offers several programs to support children who have a parent with cancer. Kids Konnected maintains a hotline, provides packets of information to children, provides referrals to local groups with monthly meetings, and helps communities start their own local support groups. The toll-free number for the Kids Konnected Hotline is 800-899-2866.

National Alliance of Breast Cancer Organizations (NABCO)

9 East 37th St.

New York, NY 10016

Phone: 212-889-0606

Web site: www.nabco.org

The National Alliance of Breast Cancer Organizations is a central resource for information and education about breast cancer. Its Web site has links to most major breast cancer organizations in the United States, and provides news and information about treatment resources and clinical trials.

National Cancer Institute (NCI)

NCI Public Inquiries Office

Building 31, Room 10A03

31 Center Dr., MSC 2580

Bethesda, MD 20892-2580

Phone: 301-435-3848

Toll-free phone for Cancer Information Service:

   800-4-CANCER (800-422-6237)

Web site: www.nci.nih.gov

A division of the National Institutes of Health, the National Cancer Institute sponsors the Cancer Information Service, a nationwide telephone service for cancer patients and their families and friends, the general public, and health care professionals. The service is free. Its staff can answer cancer-related questions in English or Spanish, as well as send free National Cancer Institute informational materials. Call 800-4-CANCER (800-422-6237). NCI booklets are also available through the Web site: www.nci.nih.gov.

OncoLink

University of Pennsylvania Cancer Center

Web site: www.oncolink.org

An online clearinghouse of cancer information, OncoLink offers comprehensive information about specific types of cancer, updates on cancer treatments, and news about research advances. The information is updated every day and provided at various levels, from introductory to in-depth.

Susan G. Komen Breast Cancer Foundation

(national office)

5005 LBJ Freeway, Suite 370

Dallas, TX 75244

Toll-free phone for hotline: 800-462-9273

Web site: www.sdkomen.org.

The Susan G. Komen Foundation funds breast cancer research, breast cancer education, and screening and treatment projects for the medically underserved. An online service of the Komen Foundation at www.breastcancerinfo.com offers comprehensive information about breast cancer. The Komen Foundation has a national toll-free Breast Care Helpline that is answered by trained volunteers whose lives have been personally touched by breast cancer. Call 800-I'M-AWARE (800-462-9273) from 9:00 A.M. to 4:30 P.M. Central Standard Time, Monday through Friday.

Y-ME National Breast Cancer Organization

212 W. Van Buren St., Suite 500
Chicago, IL 60607-3908
Phone (office): 312-986-8597
Fax: 312-294-8597
24-hour Y-ME National Breast Cancer Hotlines:
    800-221-2141 (English)
    800-986-9505 (Spanish)
Web site: www.y-me.org

Founded in 1978, the Y-ME National Breast Cancer Organization's mission is to ensure through information and peer support that no one faces breast cancer alone. Y-ME provides information and support through its 24-hour toll-free hotline, mailings, peer support groups, and Web site.

Y-ME has affiliate partners in the following states: Arizona, California, Colorado, Connecticut, District of Columbia, Illinois, Indiana, Maryland, New Jersey, New Mexico, Ohio, Oklahoma, Pennsylvania, Tennessee, Texas, Virginia, and Wisconsin.

For breast cancer information or support, call 800-221-2141 (English) or 800-986-9505 (Spanish). Call this number as well to obtain information about Y-ME's monthly one-hour teleconference program called the ShareRing Network.

GILA MONSTER

Other Books
From Imagination Press

Depression Is the Pits But I'm Getting Better:
A Guide for Adolescents
by E. Jane Garland, M.D.
For teens, this guidebook is packed with practical information, reassurance, and help for coping with and overcoming depression. For ages 12-15.

Homemade Books to Help Kids Cope
by Robert G. Ziegler.
For parents and other caregivers, this book shows how to create personalized books for and with children who need help dealing with changes, feelings, and unexpected events in their lives. For caregivers of children ages 4-13.

The Inside Story on Teen Girls
by Karen Zager, PhD, and Alice Rubenstein, EdD.
Useful tips and practical suggestions for better communication and greater understanding between parents and their teenage daughters, plus ways to reconnect with other family members and strengthen girls' sense of self. An APA LifeTools book. For both parents and teens.

My Grandma's the Mayor
by Marjorie White Pellegrino, illustrated by John Lund.
A story about character and community spirit. "One of this book's many strengths is the implication that sharing the people we love with others and giving of oneself are important to a meaningful life"—*NAPRA Review*. For ages 6-12.

Parenting That Works
by Edward R. Christopherson, PhD, and Susan L. Mortsweet, PhD.
A guidebook for parents to help their children develop character, independence, and self-confidence; offers practical advice and explains proven parenting strategies. An APA LifeTools book. For parents.

Sammy's Mommy Has Cancer
by Sherry Kohlenberg, illustrated by Lauri Crow.
A story to help young children understand and adjust to the changes in their lives when a parent is diagnosed with a life-threatening illness; includes suggested activities. For ages 3-7.

Too Nice
by Marjorie White Pellegrino, illustrated by Bonnie Matthews.
A story to illustrate appropriate assertiveness skills for young people who are afraid to stand up for themselves or express their wants and needs.
For ages 8-12.

Why Are You So Sad? A Child's Book About Parental Depression
by Beth Andrews, illustrated by Nicole Wong.
For children with a depressed parent, this book tells kids what depression is, the treatments available, and how they can cope and feel better while their parent is getting better. For ages 3-8.

MAGINATION PRESS
The American Psychological Association
750 First Street, NE
Washington, DC 20002

MAGINATION PRESS *and APA LifeTools are imprints of the American Psychological Association. For more information about our books or to place an order, please write to us, visit our website at www.apa.org or www.maginationpress.com, or call 800-374-2721.*

About the Author

Ann Speltz grew up with seven brothers and sisters in a small town on the Mississippi River in southern Minnesota. She studied literature and art at Macalester College and received her Ph.D. in English from the State University of New York at Stony Brook. She has been a university teacher and administrator, as well as an editor and developer of humanities curricula for elementary and secondary schools. After completing treatment for breast cancer in 1998, she founded Kid Support, a nonprofit organization that establishes adult-led peer support groups for the children of cancer patients. She lives with her husband and daughter in Evanston, Illinois.

About the Illustrator

Kate Sternberg grew up in western New York, where she graduated from Rochester Institute of Technology with a Bachelor's degree in fine arts and a Master's in art education. She is the author and illustrator of *Mama's Morning,* and has illustrated several other children's books, including the Phoebe Flower's Adventures series and *The Best of Brakes.* Currently, she is an art teacher at Stone Middle School in Northern Virginia, and nurturer to husband Bob, sons Ryan and Max, and several furry felines.

ACKNOWLEDGMENTS

I wish to thank my editor Darcie Johnston, whose guiding hand made *The Year My Mother Was Bald* the best it could possibly be. I would also like to acknowledge the Anderson Center for Interdisciplinary Studies at Tower View, whose residency program provided me with a quiet place to retreat while writing the first draft of this book. Finally, I want to thank my husband, Stephen Fedo, for his enthusiastic support of this project, and for his editorial suggestions at every stage of the writing and revision process.

PICTURE CREDITS